Michael Bruce

**Poems On Several Occasions**

Michael Bruce

**Poems On Several Occasions**

ISBN/EAN: 9783742814432

Manufactured in Europe, USA, Canada, Australia, Japa

Cover: Foto ©Andreas Hilbeck / pixelio.de

Manufactured and distributed by brebook publishing software
(www.brebook.com)

Michael Bruce

**Poems On Several Occasions**

# P O E M S.

## ON

## SEVERAL OCCASIONS.

### BY

### MICHAEL BRUCE.

*——Sine me, liber, ibis in urbem.* OVID.

EDINBURGH:

PRINTED BY J. ROBERTSON;

FOR W. ANDERSON, BOOKSELLER, STIRLING

M DCC LXXXII.

# P R E F A C E.

MICHAEL BRUCE, the Author of the following Poems, lives now no more but in the remembrance of his friends. He was born in a remote village in KINROSS ſhire, and deſcended from parents remarkable for nothing but the innocence and ſimplicity of their lives. They, however, had the penetration to diſcover in their young ſon a genius ſuperior to the common, and had the merit to give him a polite and liberal education. From his earlieſt years, he had

manifeſted .

manifested the most sanguine love of let-
ters, and afterwards made eminent progrefs in many branches of literature. But
poetry was his darling study; the poets
were his perpetual companions. He read
their works with avidity, and with a con-
genial enthusiasm; he caught their spirit
as well as their manner; and though he
fometimes imitated their style, he was a
poet from inspiration. No lefs amiable
as a man, than valuable as a writer; en-
dued with good nature, and good senfe;
humane, friendly, benevolent; he loved
his friends, and was beloved by them with
a degree of ardour that is only experien-
ced in the æra of youth and innocence.

It

It was during the ſummer vacations of the college that he compoſed the follow-ing Poems. If images of nature that are beautiful and new; if ſentiments, warm from the heart, intereſting, and pathetic; if a ſtyle, chaſte with ornament, and ele-gant with ſimplicity; if theſe, and many other beauties of nature and of art, are allowed to conſtitute true poetic merit, the following Poems will ſtand high in the judgment of men of taſte.

AFTER the author had finiſhed his courſe of philoſophy at EDINBURGH, he was ſeized with a conſumption, of which he died, about the 21ſt year of his age.

DURING

DURING that difeafe, and in the immediate view of death, he wrote the elegy which concludes this collection; the latter part of which is wrought up into the moft paffionate ftrains of the true pathetic, and is not perhaps inferior to any poetry in any language.

To make up a mifcellany, fome poems, wrote by different authors, are inferted, all of them original, and none of them deftitute of merit. The reader of tafte will eafily diftinguifh them from thofe of MR BRUCE, without their being particularized by any mark.

SEVERAL

SEVERAL of thefe Poems have been approved by perfons of the firft tafte in
the kingdom, and the Editor publifhes
them to that fmall circle for whom they
are intended, not with folicitude and
anxiety, but with the pleafurable re-
flection that he is furnifhing out a claffi-
cal entertainment to every reader of refi-
ned tafte.

# CONTENTS.

# CONTENTS.

B          *The Muſiad :*

POEMS.

# P O E M S

## O N

# SEVERAL OCCASIONS.

## T H E

# EAGLE, CROW, AND SHEPHERD:

### A FABLE.

BENEATH the horror of a rock,
  A fhepherd carelefs fed his flock.
Soufe from its top an eagle came,
And feiz'd upon a fporting lamb;
Its tender fides his talons tear,
And bear it bleating thro' the air.

Thro

THIS was difcover'd by a crow,
Who hopp'd upon the plain below.
" You ram," fays he, " becomes my prey;"
And, mounting, haftens to the fray,
Lights on his back—when lo, ill-luck !
He in the fleece entangled ftuck ;
He fpreads his wings, but can't get free,
Struggling in vain for liberty.

THE fhepherd foon the captive fpies,
And foon he feizes on the prize.
His children curious croud around,
And afk what ftrange fowl he has found?
" My fons," faid he, " warn'd by this wretch,
" Attempt no deed above your reach :
" An eagle not an hour ago,
" He's now content to be a crow."

ALEXIS:

## ALEXIS: A PASTORAL.

UPON a bank with cowflips cover'd o'er,
 Where LEVEN's waters break againſt the ſhore;
What time the village fires in circles talk,
And youths and maidens take their evening walk;
Among the yellow broom ALEXIS lay,
And view'd the beauties of the ſetting day.

FULL well you might obſerve ſome inward ſmart,
Some ſecret grief hung heavy at his heart.
While round the field his ſportive lambkins play'd,
He rais'd his plaintive voice, and thus he ſaid:

BEGIN, my pipe! a ſoftly mournful ſtrain.
The parting ſun ſhines yellow on the plain;
The balmy weſt-wind breathes along the ground;
Their evening ſweets the flow'rs diſpenſe around;

The

The flocks ſtray bleating o'er the mountain's brow,

And from the plain the anſw'ring cattle low ;

Sweet chant the feather'd tribes on every tree,

And all things feel the joys of love, but me.


BEGIN, my pipe ! begin the mournful ſtrain.

EUMELIA meets my kindneſs with diſdain.

Oft have I try'd her ſtubborn heart to move,

And in her icy boſom kindle love :

But all in vain—ere I my love declar'd,

With other youths her company I ſhar'd ;

But now ſhe ſhuns me hopeleſs and forlorn,

And pays my conſtant paſſion with her ſcorn.


BEGIN, my pipe ! the ſadly-ſoothing ſtrain,

And bring the days of innocence again.

Well I remember, in the funny ſcene

We ran, we play'd together on the green.

Fair

Fair in our youth, and wanton in our play,

We toy'd, we fported the long fummer's day.

For her I fpoil'd the gardens of the fpring,

And taught the goldfinch on her hand to fing.

We fat and fung beneath the lovers tree ;

One was her look, and it was fix'd on me.


BEGIN, my pipe ! a melancholy ftrain.

A holiday was kept on yonder plain ;

The feaft was fpread upon the flow'ry mead,

And fkilful THYRSIS tun'd his vocal reed ;

Each for the dance felects the nymph he loves,

And every nymph with fmiles her fwain approves :

The fetting fun beheld their mirthful glee,

And left all happy in their love, but me.


BEGIN, my pipe ! a foftly-mournful ftrain.

O cruel nymph ! O moft unhappy fwain !

To

To climb the fteepy rock's tremendous height,
And crop its herbage is the goats delight;
The flowery thyme delights the humming bees,
And blooming wilds the bleating lambkins pleafe;
DAPHNIS courts CHLOE under every tree:
EUMELIA! you alone have joys for me!


Now ceafe, my pipe! now ceafe the mournful ftrain.
Lo, yonder comes EUMELIA o'er the plain!
Till fhe approach, I'll lurk behind the fhade,
Then try with all my art the ftubborn maid:
Though to her lover cruel and unkind,
Yet time may change the purpofe of her mind.
But vain thefe pleafing hopes! already fee,
She hath obferv'd, and now fhe flies from me!

THEN

THEN ceafe, my pipe! the unavailing ftrain.

APOLLO aids, the Nine infpire in vain :

You, cruel maid! refufe to lend an ear ;

No more I fing, fince you difdain to hear.

This pipe AMYNTAS gave, on which he play'd :

" Be thou its fecond lord," the dying fhepherd faid.

No more I play, now filent let it be ;

Nor pipe, nor fong, can e'er give joy to me.


# DAMON, MENALCAS, AND
# MELIBOEUS.

## AN ECLOGUE.

### DAMON.

MILD from the fhower, the morning's rofy light
Unfolds the beauteous feafon to the fight :

C '                                        The

The landfcape rifes verdant on the view ;
The little hills uplift their heads in dew ;
The funny ftream rejoices in the vale;
The woods with fongs approaching fummer hail :
The boy comes forth among the flow'rs to play;
His fair hair glitters in the yellow ray.
Shepherds, begin the fong! while, o'er the mead,
Your flocks at will on dewy paftures feed.
Behold fair nature, and begin the fong ;
The fongs of nature to the fwain belong,
Who equals Cona's bard in filvan ftrains,
To him his harp an equal prize remains;
His harp, which founds on all its facred ftrings
The loves of hunters, and the wars of kings.

### MENALCAS.

Now fleecy clouds in clearer fkies are feen ;
The air is genial, and the earth is green :

O'er

O'er hill and dale the flow'rs fpontaneous fpring,

And blackbirds finging now invite to fing.

### MELIBOEUS.

Now milky fhow'rs rejoice the fpringing grain;

New-opening pea-blooms purple all the plain;

The hedges bloffom white on every hand;

Already harveft feems to clothe the land.

### MENALCAS.

White o'er the hill my fnowy fheep appear,

Each with her lamb; their fhepherds name they bear.

I love to lead them where the daifies fpring,

And on the funny hill to fit and fing.

### MELIBOEUS.

My fields are green with clover and with corn;

My flocks the hills, and herds the vales adorn.

I teach the ftream, I teach the vocal fhore,

And woods to echo that "I want no more."

MENALCAS.

### MENALCAS.

To me the bees their annual nectar yield;
Peace cheers my hut, and plenty clothes my field.
I fear no lofs: I give to Ocean's wind
All care away, a monarch in my mind.

### MELIBOEUS.

My mind is cheerful as the linnet's lays;
Heav'n daily hears a fhepherd's fimple praife.
What time I fhear my flock, I fend a fleece
To aged MOPSA, and her orphan niece.

### MENALCAS.

LAVINIA, come! here primrofes upfpring;
Here choirs of linnets, here yourfelf may fing;
Here meadows worthy of thy foot appear:
O come, LAVINIA! let us wander here!

### MELIBOEUS.

ROSELLA, come! here flow'rs the heath adorn;
Here ruddy rofes open on the thorn;

Here

Here willows by the brook a fhadow give ;

O here, ROSELLA ! let us love to live !

#### MENALCAS.

LAVINIA's fairer than the flow'rs of May,

Or Autumn apples ruddy in the ray :

For her my flow'rs are in a garland wove,

And all my apples ripen for my love.

#### MELIBOEUS.

PRINCE of the wood, the oak majeftic tow'rs ;

The lily of the vale is queen of flow'rs :

Above the maids ROSELLA's charms prevail,

As oaks in woods, and lilies in the vale.

#### MENALCAS.

RESOUND, ye rocks ! ye little hills ! rejoice !

Affenting woods ! to Heaven uplift your voice !

Let Spring and Summer enter hand in hand ;

LAVINIA comes, the glory of our land !

#### MELIBOEUS.

### MELIBOEUS.

Whene'er my love appears upon the plain,

To her the wond'ring fhepherds tune the ftrain:

" Who comes in beauty like the vernal morn,

" When yellow robes of light all heaven and earth

" adorn."

### MENALCAS.

Rosella's mine, by all the Pow'rs above;

Each ftar in heav'n is witnefs to our love.

Among the lilies fhe abides all day;

Herfelf as lovely, and as fweet as they.

### MELIBOEUS.

By Tweed Lavinia feeds her fleecy care,

And in the fun-fhine combs her yellow hair.

Be thine the peace of Heav'n, unknown to kings,

And o'er thee angels fpread their guardian wings!

MENALCAS.

### MENALCAS.

I followed Nature, and was fond of praife ;

Thrice noble Varo has approved my lays;

If he approves, fuperior to my peers,

I join th' immortal choir, and fing to other years.

### MELIBOEUS.

My miftrefs is my Mufe : the banks of Tyne

Refound with Nature's mufic, and with mine ;

Helen the fair, the beauty of our green,

To me adjudg'd the prize when chofen queen.

### DAMON.

Now ceafe your fongs : the flocks to fhelter fly,

And the high fun has gain'd the middle fky.

To both alike the poet's bays belong,

· Chiefs of the choir, and mafters of the fong.

Thus let your pipes contend, with rival ftrife,

To fing the praifes of the paftoral life :

Sing

Sing Nature's fcenes with Nature's beauties fir'd,

Where poets dream'd, where prophets lay infpir'd.

Even CALEDONIAN queens have trod the meads,

And fcepter'd kings affum'd the fhepherds weeds :

Th' angelic choirs, that guard the throne of GOD,

Have fat with fhepherds on the humble fod.

With us renew'd the golden times remain,

And long-loft innocence is found again.

# PASTORAL SONG.

*To the tune of the Yellow-hair'd Laddie.*

IN May when the gowans appear on the green,

  And flow'rs in the field and the foreft are feen ;

Where lilies bloom'd bonny, and hawthorns upfprung,

The Yellow-hair'd laddie oft whiftled and fung.

BUT

## II.

But neither the shades, nor the sweets of the flow'rs,
Nor the blackbirds that warbled on blossoming bow'rs,
Could pleasure his eye, or his ear entertain ;
For love was his pleasure, and love was his pain.

## III.

The shepherd thus sung, while his flocks all around
Drew nearer and nearer, and sigh'd to the sound :
Around as in chains, lay the beasts of the wood,
With pity disarmed, with music subdu'd.

## IV.

Young Jessy is fair as the spring's early flower,
And Mary sings sweet as the bird in her bower :
But Peggy is fairer and sweeter than they ;
With looks like the morning, with smiles like the day.

## V.

In the flower of her youth, in the bloom of eighteen,
Of virtue the goddess, of beauty the queen :

D           One

One hour in her prefence an æra excels
Amid courts, where ambition with mifery dwells.

### VI.

FAIR to the fhepherd the new-fpringing flow'rs,
When May and when morning lead on the gay hours:
But PEGGY is brighter and fairer than they;
She's fair as the morning, and lovely as May.

### VII.

SWEET to the fhepherd the wild woodland found,
When larks fing above him, and lambs bleat around;
But PEGGY far fweeter can fpeak and can fing,
Than the notes of the warblers that welcome the fpring.

### VIII.

WHEN in beauty fhe moves by the brook of the plain,
You would call her a VENUS new fprung from the main:
When fhe fings, and the woods with their echoes reply,
You would think that an angel was warbling on high.

Ye

## IX.

YE Pow'rs that preside over mortal estate!
Whose nod ruleth Nature, whose pleasure is Fate,
O grant me, O grant me the heav'n of her charms!
May I live in her presence, and die in her arms!

# ECLOGUE.

*In the manner of* OSSIAN.

O COME, my love! from thy echoing hill; thy
locks on the mountain wind!

THE hill-top flames with setting light; the vale is
bright with the beam of eve. Blithe on the village
green the maiden milks her cows. The boy shouts in
the wood, and wonders who talks from the trees. But

D 2                                          Echo

Ecko talks from the trees, repeating his notes of joy. Where art thou, O MORNA! thou faireft among women? I hear not the bleating of thy flock, nor thy voice in the wind of the hill. Here is the field of our loves; now is the hour of thy promife. See, frequent from the harveft-field the reapers eye the fetting fun: but thou appeareft not on the plain.----

DAUGHTERS of the bow! Saw ye my love, with her little flock tripping before her? Saw ye her, fair moving over the heath, and waving her locks behind like the yellow fun-beams of evening?

COME from the hill of clouds, fair dweller of woody LUMON!

I

I WAS a boy when I went to Lumon's lovely vale. Sporting among the willows of the brook, I faw the daughters of the plain.   Fair were their faces of youth; but mine eye was fixed on MORNA.   Red was her cheek, and fair her hair.   Her hand was white as the lily.   Mild was the beam of her blue eye, and lovely as the laft fmile of the fun.   Her eye met mine in filence.   Sweet were our words together in fecret.   I little knew what meant the heavings of my bofom, and the wild wifh of my heart.   I often looked back upon Lumon's vale, and bleft the fair dwelling of MORNA.   Her name dwelt ever on my lip.   She came to my dream by night.   Thou didft come in thy beauty, O maid! lovely as the ghoft of MALVINA, when, clad with the robes of heaven, fhe came to the vale of the Moon, to vifit the aged eyes of OSSIAN king of harps.

COME

COME from the cloud of night, thou first of our maidens! come ——

THE wind is down; the sky is clear: red is the cloud of evening. In circles the bat wheels over head; the boy purfues his flight. The farmer hails the figns of heaven, the promife of halcyon days: Joy brightens in his eyes. O MORNA! firft of maidens! thou art the joy of SALGAR! thou art his one defire! I wait thy coming on the field. Mine eye is over all the plain. One echo fpreads on every fide. It is the fhout of the fhepherds folding their flocks. They call to their companions, each on his echoing hill. From the red cloud rifes the evening ftar.— But who comes yonder in light, like the Moon the queen of heaven? It is fhe! the ftar of ftars! the lovely light of LUMON! Welcome, fair beam of beauty, for ever to fhine in our valleys!

MORNA.

## MORNA.

I Come from the hill of clouds. Among the green
rushes of BALVA's bank, I follow the steps of my beloved. The foal in the meadow frolics round the
mare : his bright mane dances on the mountain wind.
The leverets play among the green ferns, fearless of
the hunter's horn, and of the bounding gray-hound.
The last strain is up in the wood.---Did I hear the
voice of my love? It was the gale that sports with
the whirling leaf, and sighs in the reeds of the lake.
Blessed be the voice of winds that brings my SALGAR
to mind. O SALGAR! youth of the rolling eye!
thou art the love of maidens. Thy face is a sun to
thy friends : thy words are sweet as a song : thy
steps are stately on thy hill : thou art comely in the
brightness of youth ; like the Moon, when she puts
off her dun robe in the sky, and brightens the face of
night. The clouds rejoice on either side: the tra-
veller

veller in the narrow path beholds her, round, in her beauty moving through the midft of heaven. Thou art fair, O youth of the rolling eye! thou waft the love of my youth.

### SALGAR.

. FAIR wanderer of evening! pleafant be thy reft on our plains. I was gathering nuts in the wood for my love, and the days of our youth returned to mind; when we played together on the green, and flew over the field with feet of wind. I tamed the blackbird for my love, and taught it to fing in her hand. I climbed the afh in the cliff of the rock, and brought you the doves of the wood.

### MORNA.

IT is the voice of my beloved! Let me behold him from the wood-covered vale, as he fings of the times of old, and complains to the voice of the rock. Pleafant were the days of our youth, like the fongs of

other

other years. Often have we fat on the old grey ftone, and filent marked the ftars, as one by one they ftole into the fky. One was our wifh by day, and one our dream by night.

### SALGAR.

I FOUND an apple-tree in the wood. I planted it in my garden. Thine eye beheld it all in flower. Fcr every bloom we marked, I count an apple of gold. To-morrow I pull the fruit for you. O come, my beft beloved.

### MORNA.

WHEN the goffamour melts in air, and the furze crackle in the beam of noon, O come to CONA's funny fide, and let thy flocks wander in our valleys. The heath is in flower. One tree rifes in the midft. Sweet flows the river by its fide of age. The wild bee hides his honey at its root. Our words will be fweet on

E                                      the

the funny hill.   Till grey Evening fhadow the plain,
I will fing to my well-beloved.

# D A P H N I S:

## A  M O N O D Y.

*To the memory of a Young Boy of great parts.*

NO more of youthful joys or love's fond dreams,
   No more of morning fair, or ev'ning mild,
While DAPHNIS lies among the filent dead
Unfung; tho' long ago he trod the path,
The dreary road of death ——
Which foon or late each human foot muft tread:
He trod the dark uncomfortable wild
By Faith's pure light, by Hope's heav'n-op'ning beams,
By Love whofe image gladdens mortal eyes,
And keeps the golden key that opens all the fkies.

ASSIST

## II.

Assist, ye Mufes!—and ye will affift;
For Daphnis, whom I fing, to you was dear:
Ye lov'd the boy, and on his youthful head
Your kindeft influence fhed.—
So may I match his lays, who to the lyre
Wail'd his loft Lycidas by wood and rill:
So may the Mufe my grov'ling mind infpire
To fing a farewell to thy afhes bleft;
To bid fair peace be to thy gentle fhade;
To fcatter flow'rets, cropt by Fancy's hand,
In fad affemblage round thy tomb,
If water'd by the Mufe, to lateft time to bloom.

## III.

Oft by the fide of Leven's cryftal lake,
Trembling beneath the clofing lids of light,
With flow fhort-meafur'd fteps we took our walk:
Then he would talk

Of

Of argument far, far above his years;

Then he would reafon high,

'Till from the eaſt the ſilver Queen of night

Her journey up heav'n's ſteep began to make,

And Silence reign'd attentive in the ſky.

### IV.

O HAPPY days! for ever, ever gone!

When o'er the flow'ry green we ran, we play'd

With blooms bedropt by youthful Summer's hand;

Or, in the willow-ſhade,

We mimic caſtles built among the ſand,

Soon by the founding ſurge to be beat down,

Or ſweeping winds; when, by the ſedgy marſh,

We heard the heron, and the wild duck harſh,

And ſweeter lark tune his melodious lay,

At higheſt noon of day.

Among the antic moſs-grown ſtones we'd roam,

With ancient hieroglyphic figures grac'd,

Winged

Winged hour-glaffes, bones, and fkulls, and fpades,

And obfolete infcriptions by the hands

Of other ages; ah! I little thought

That we then play'd o'er his untimely tomb!

### V.

WHERE were ye, Mufes! when the leaden hand

Of Death, remorfelefs, clos'd your DAPHNIS' eyes?

For fure ye heard the weeping mother's cries;

But the dread pow'r of Fate what can withftand?

Young DAPHNIS fmil'd at Death; the tyrant's darts

As ftubble counted.   What was his fupport?

His confcience, and firm truft in him whofe ways

Are truth; in him who fways

His potent fceptre o'er the dark domains

Of death and hell; who holds in ftrait'ned reins

Their banded legions: " Thro' the darkfome vale

" He'll guide my trembling fteps with heav'nly ray;

" I fee the dawning of immortal day,"

D 2                                   " He

He smiling said, and died !—

### VI.

Hail and farewell, blest youth! soon hast thou left
This evil world; fair was thy thread of life,
But quickly by the envious Sisters shorn :
Thus have I seen a rose with rising morn
Unfold its glowing bloom, sweet to the smell,
And lovely to the eye ; when a keen wind
Hath tore its blushing leaves, and laid it low,
Stripp'd of its sweets.—Ah ! so,
So Daphnis fell! long ere his prime he fell !
Nor left he on these plains his peer behind ;
These plains, that mourn their loss, of him bereft,
No more look gay, but desert and forlorn.

### VII.

Now cease your lamentations, shepherds! cease :
Tho' Daphnis died below, he lives above ;
A better life, and in a fairer clime,   .

He

He lives : no forrow enters that bleft place,

But ceafelefs fongs of love and joy refound ;

And fragrance floats around,

By fanning zephyrs from the fpicy groves,

And flow'rs immortal, wafted ; Afphodel

And Amaranth, unfading, deck the ground,

With fairer colours than, ere ADAM fell,

In EDEN bloom'd : there hap'ly he may hear,

This artlefs fong.   Ye pow'rs of verfe ! improve,

And make it worthy of your darling's ear,

And make it equal to the fhepherd's love.

### VIII.

THUS, in the fhadow of a frowning rock, .   .

Beneath a mountain's fide, fhaggy and hoar,

A homely fwain tending his little flock,

Rude, yet a lover of the Mufe's lore,

Chanted his Doric ftrain till clofe of day,

Then rofe, and homeward flowly bent his way.

SIR

## SIR JAMES THE ROSS.

### AN HISTORICAL BALLAD.

OF all the Scottish northern Chiefs
    Of high and mighty name,
The bravest was Sir JAMES THE ROSS,
    A knight of meikle fame.


His growth was like a youthful oak,
    That crowns the mountain's brow;
And, waving o'er his shoulders broad,
    His locks of yellow flew.


Wide were his fields, his herds were large,
    And large his flocks of sheep,
And num'rous were his goats and deer
    Upon the mountains steep.

The chieftain of the good Clan Ross,
  A firm and warlike band :
Five hundred warriors drew the sword
  Beneath his high command.

In bloody fight thrice had he stood
  Against the English keen,
Ere two and twenty op'ning springs
  The blooming youth had seen.

The fair Matilda dear he lov'd,
  A maid of beauty rare ;
Even Marg'ret on the Scottish throne
  Was never half so fair.

Long had he woo'd, long she refus'd
  With seeming scorn and pride ;
Yet oft her eyes confess'd the love
  Her fearful words deny'd.

F

As

At length fhe blefs'd his well-try'd love,
　　Allow'd his tender claim ;
She vow'd to him her virgin-heart,
　　And own'd an equal flame.


Her brother, BUCHAN's cruel lord,
　　Their paffion difapprov'd :
He bade her wed Sir JOHN the GRÆME,
　　And leave the youth fhe lov'd.


One night they met, as they were wont,
　　Deep in a fhady wood ;
Where on the bank, befide the burn,
　　A blooming faugh-tree ftood.


Conceal'd among the underwood
　　The crafty DONALD lay,
The brother of Sir JOHN the GRÆME,
　　To watch what they might fay.

Wheu

When thus the maid began : " My Sire

 " Our paſſion diſapproves ;

" He bids me wed Sir JOHN the GRÆME,

 " So here muſt end our loves.

" My father's will muſt be obey'd,

 " Nought boots me to withſtand ;

" Some fairer maid in beauty's bloom

 " Shall bleſs thee with her hand.

" Soon will MATILDA be forgot,

 " And from thy mind effac'd ;

" But may that happineſs be thine,

 " Which I can never taſte !"

" What do I hear ? Is this thy vow ?"

 Sir JAMES the Ross replied ;

" And will MATILDA wed the GRÆME,

 " Tho' ſworn to be my bride ?

      " His

" His fword fhall fooner pierce my heart,

" Than reave me of thy charms"——

And clafp'd her to his throbbing breaft,

Faſt lock'd within her arms.


" I fpoke to try thy love," fhe faid, .

" I'll near wed man but thee ;

" The grave fhall be my bridal bed,

" If Græme my hufband be.


" Take then, dear youth ! this faithful kifs,.

" In witnefs of my troth ;

" And every plague become my lot,

" That day I break my oath."


They parted thus—the fun was fet:

Up hafty Donald flies ;

And, " Turn thee, turn thee, beardlefs youth !"

He loud infulting cries.

Soon

Soon turn'd about the fearlefs chief,
　　And foon his fword he drew ;
For DONALD's blade before his breaft
　　Had pierc'd his tartans thro'.

" This for my brother's flighted love :
　　" His wrongs fit on my arm."—
Three paces back the youth retir'd,
　　And fav'd himfelf from harm.

Returning fwift, his fword he rear'd
　　Fierce DONALD's head above ;
And thro' the brain and crafhing bone
　　The furious weapon drove.

Life iffued at the wound ; he fell,
　　A lump of lifelefs clay :
" So fall my foes," quoth valiant ROSS,
　　And ftately ftrode away.

　　　　　　　　　　　　　　　Thro'

Thro' the green wood in hafte he pafs'd

    Unto Lord BUCHAN's hall,

Beneath MATILDA's windows ftood,

    And thus on her did call :

" Art thou afleep, MATILDA fair !

    " Awake, my love ! awake ;

" Behold thy lover waits without,

    " A long farewell to take.

" For I have flain fierce DONALD GRÆME,

    " His blood is on my fword ;

" And far, far diftant are my men,

    " Nor can defend their lord.

" To SKYE I will direct my flight,

    " Where my brave brothers bide,

" And raife the Mighty of the Ifles

    " To combat on my fide."

" O do not ſo," the maid replied,

 " With me till morning ſtay;

" For dark and dreary is the night,

 " And dang'rous is the way.


" All night I'll watch thee in the park;

 " My faithful page I'll ſend,

" In haſte to raiſe the brave Clan Ross

 " Their maſter to defend."


He laid him down beneath a buſh,

 And wrap'd him in his plaid;

While, trembling for her lover's fate,

 At diſtance ſtood the maid.


Swift ran the page o'er hill and dale,

 Till, in a lowly glen,

He met the furious Sir JOHN GRÆME

 With twenty of his men,

        " Where

" Where goeſt ? thou little page !" he ſaid,

　" So late who did thee ſend ?"

" I go to raiſe the brave Clan Ross,

　" Their maſter to defend.

" For he has ſlain fierce Donald Græme,

　" His blood is on his ſword ;

" And far, far diſtant are his men,

　" Nor can aſſiſt their lord."

" And has he ſlain my brother dear ?"

　The furious chief replies :

" Diſhonour blaſt my name, but he

　" By me ere morning dies.

" Say, page ! where is Sir James the Ross ?

　" I will thee well reward."

" He ſleeps into Lord Buchan's park ;

　" Matilda is his guard."

They

They fpurr'd their fteeds, and furious flew,
    Like light'ning, o'er the lea :
They reach'd Lord BUCHAN's lofty tow'rs
    By dawning of the day.

MATILDA ftood without the gate
    Upon a rifing ground,
And watch'd each object in the dawn,
    All ear to every found.

" Where fleeps the Ross ?" began the GRÆME,
    " Or has the felon fled ?
" This hand fhall lay the wretch on earth,
    " By whom my brother bled."

And now the valiant knight awoke,
    The virgin fhrieking heard :
Straight up he rofe, and drew his fword,
    When the fierce band appear'd.

G                  " Your

" Your fword laft night my brother flew,

" His blood yet dims its fhine ;

" And, ere the fun fhall gild the morn,

" Your blood fhall reek on mine."


" Your words are brave," the chief return'd ;

" But deeds approve the man.

" Set by your men, and hand to hand

" We'll try what valour can."


With dauntlefs ftep he forward ftrode,

And dar'd him to the fight :

The GRÆME gave back, and fear'd his arm,

For well he knew his might.


Four of his men, the braveft four,

Sunk down beneath his fword ;

But ftill he fcorn'd the poor revenge,

And fought their haughty lord.

Behind

Behind him bafely came the GRÆME,
　　And wounded in the fide :
Out fpouting came the purple ftream,
　　And all his tartans dy'd.


But yet his hand not dropp'd the fword,
　　Nor funk he to the ground,
Till thro' his en'my's heart his fword
　　Had forc'd a mortal wound.


GRÆME, like a tree by winds o'erthrown,
　　Fell breathlefs on the clay ;
And down befide him funk the Ross,
　　And faint and dying lay.


MATILDA faw, and faft fhe ran :
　　" O fpare his life," fhe cried ;
" Lord BUCHAN's daughter begs his life,
　　" Let her not be denied."

　　　　　　　　　　Her

Her well-known voice the hero heard ;
    He rais'd his death-clos'd eyes ;
He fix'd them on the weeping maid,
    And weakly thus replies :

" In vain MATILDA begs the life
    " By death's arreſt deny'd ;
" My race is run—adieu, my love !"
    Then clos'd his eyes, and dy'd.

The ſword, yet warm from his left ſide,
    With frantic hand ſhe drew ;
" I come, Sir JAMES the Ross," ſhe cry'd,
    " I come to follow you."

The hilt ſhe lean'd againſt the ground,
    And bar'd her ſnowy breaſt,
Then fell upon her lover's face,
    And ſunk to endleſs reſt.

                                   V E R N A L

# VERNAL ODE.

SEE! fee! the genial Spring again;
   Unbind the glebe, and paint the plain.
The garden blooms: the tulips gay
For thee put on their beft array,
And ev'ry flower fo richly dight
In fpangled robes of varying light.

FROM noify towns and noxious fky,
Hither, AMELIA! hafte and fly.
View thefe gay fcenes, their fweets inhale;
Health breathes in every balmy gale;
Nor fear left the returning ftorm
The vernal feafon may deform.
For hark! I hear the fwallows fing,
Who ne'er uncertain tidings bring:

They

They with glad voice proclaim on high,

" The Spring is come, the Summer's nigh."

Sweet bird ! what facred lore is thine,

The change of feafons to divine ?

Thou counteft no revolving day

By folar or fidereal ray :

No clock haft thou, with bufy chime

To tell the filent lapfe of time,

To call thee from thy drowfy cell ;

'Tis heaven that rings thy matin bell.

Strait all the chatt'ring tribe obey,

Start from their trance, and wing away ;

To their lov'd fummer feats repair,

And ev'ry pinion floats on air.

ODE.

## ODE: TO A FOUNTAIN.

O Fountain of the wood! whofe glaffy wave
    Slow-welling from the rock of years,
      Holds to heav'n a mirrour blue,
        And bright as ANNA's eye,


With whom I've fported on the margin green:
    My hand with leaves, with lilies white,
      Gaily deck'd her golden hair,
        Young NAIAD of the vale.


Fount of my native wood! thy murmurs greet
    My ear, like poets heav'nly ftrain:
      Fancy pictures in a dream
        The golden days of youth.

                      O ftate

O ſtate of innocence! O paradiſe!
  In Hope's gay garden, Fancy views
    Golden bloſſoms, golden fruits,
      And EDEN ever green.

Where now, ye dear companions of my youth!
  Ye brothers of my boſom! where
    Do ye tread the walks of life,
      Wide ſcatter'd o'er the world?

Thus winged larks forſake their native neſt,
  The merry minſtrels of the morn;
    New to heav'n they mount away,
      And meet again no more.

All things decay; the foreſt like the leaf;
  Great kingdoms fall; the peopled globe,
    Planet-ſtruck, ſhall paſs away;
      Heav'ns with their hoſts expire:

                                    But

But Hope's fair vifions, and the beams of Joy,

    Shall cheer my befom : I will fing

        Nature's beauty, Nature's birth,

           And heroes on the lyre.


Ye Naiads ! blue-eyed fifters of the wood !

    Who by old oak, or ftoried ftream,

        Nightly tread your myftic maze,

           And charm the wand'ring Moon,


Beheld by poet's eye ; infpire my dreams

    With vifions, like the landfcapes fair

        Of heav'n's blifs, to dying faints

           By guardian angels drawn.


Fount of the foreft ! in thy poet's lays

    Thy waves fhall flow : this wreath of flow'rs,

        Gather'd by my Anna's hand,

           I afk to bind my brow.

               H        DANISH

# DANISH ODE.

THE great, the glorious deed is done!
   The foe is fled! the field is won!
Prepare the feaſt; the heroes call;
Let joy, let triumph fill the hall!

  THE raven claſps his ſable wings;
The Bard his choſen timbrel brings;
Six virgins round, a ſelect choir,
Sing to the muſic of his lyre.

  WITH mighty ale the goblet crown;
With mighty ale your ſorrows drown;
To-day, to mirth and joy we yield;
To morrow, face the bloody field.

FROM

FROM danger's front, at battle's eve,

Sweet comes the banquet to the brave ;

Joy fhines with genial beam on all,

The joy that dwells in ODIN's hall.


THE fong burfts living from the lyre,

Like dreams that guardian ghofts infpire ;

When mimic fhrieks the heroes hear,

And whirl the vifionary fpear.


MUSIC's the med'cine of the mind ;

The cloud of Care give to the wind ;

Be ev'ry brow with garlands bound,

And let the cup of Joy go round.


THE cloud comes o'er the beam of light ;

We're guefts that tarry but a night :

In the dark houfe, together prefs'd,.

The prince's and the people reft.

SEND round the fhell, the feaft prolong,

And fend away the night in fong ;

Be bleft below, as thofe above

With ODIN's and the friends they love.

# DANISH ODE.

I N deeds of arms, our fathers rife

Illuftrious in their offspring's eyes :

They fearlefs rufh'd thro' Ocean's ftorms,

And dar'd grim Death in all its forms ;

Each youth affum'd the fword and fhield,

And grew a hero in the field.

SHALL

SHALL we degenerate from our race,
Inglorious, in the mountain chace ?
Arm, arm in fallen HUBBA's right ;
Place your forefathers in your fight ;
To fame, to glory fight your way,
And teach the nations to obey.


ASSUME the oars, unbind the fails ;
Send, ODIN ! fend propitious gales.
At LODA's ftone, we will adore
Thy name with fongs, upon the fhore ;
And, full of thee, undaunted dare
The foe, and dart the bolts of war.


No feaft of fhells, no dance by night,
Are glorious ODIN's dear delight :
He, king of men, his armies led,
Where heroes ftrove, where battles bled ;

Now

Now reigns above the morning-ftar,

The god of thunder and of war.


Bless'd who in battle bravely fall!

They mount on wings to Odin's hall;

To Mufic's found, in cups of gold,

They drink new wine with chiefs of old;

The fong of Bards records their name,

And future times fhall fpeak their fame.


Hark! Odin thunders! hafte on board;

Illuftrious Canute! give the word.

On wings of wind we pafs the feas,

To conquer realms, if Odin pleafe:

With Odin's fpirit in our foul,

We'll gain the globe from pole to pole.


ANACREONTIC:

# ANACREONTIC:

## TO A WASP.

*The following is a ludicrous imitation of the usual A-
nacreontics ; the spirit of composing which was ra-
ging, a few years ago, among all the sweet singers of*
GREAT BRITAIN.

WINGED wand'rer of the sky !
 Inhabitant of heav'n high !
Dreadful with thy dragon tail,
Hydra-head, and cot of mail !
Why dost thou my peace molest ?
Why dost thou disturb my rest ?
When in May the meads are seen,
Sweet enamel ! white and green ;
And the gardens, and the bow'rs,
And the forests, and the flow'rs,

Don their robes of curious dye,

Fine confusion to the eye !

Did I —— chafe the in thy flight ?

Did I —— put thee in a fright ?

Did I —— spoil thy treasure hid ?

Never—never—never—did.

Envious nothing ! pray beware ;

Tempt mine anger, if you dare,

Trust not in thy strength of wing ;

Trust not in thy length of sting.

Heav'n nor earth shall thee defend ;

I thy buzzing soon will end.

Take my counsel, while you may ;

Devil take you, if you stay.

Wilt—thou—dare—my—face—to—wound ?—

Thus, I fell thee to the ground.

Down amongst the dead men, now

'Thou shalt forget thou ere waft thou.

Anacreontic

Anacreontic Bards beneath,

Thus shall wail thee after death.

## CHORUS OF ELYSIAN BARDS.

" A Wasp, for a wonder,

" To paradise under

" Descends: see ! he wanders

" By STYX's meanders !

" Behold, how he glows,

" Amidst RHODOPE's snows

" He sweats, in a trice,

" In the regions of ice !

" Lo ! he cools, by GOD's ire,

" Amidst brimstone and fire !

" He goes to our king,

" And he shows him his sting.

I                            " (God

" (God Pluto loves fatire,

" As women love attire ;)

" Our king fets him free,

" Like fam'd Euridice.

" Thus a Wafp could prevail

" O'er the Devil and hell,

" A conqueft both hard and laborious !

" Tho' hell had faft bound him,

" And the Devil did confound him,

" Yet his fting and his wing were victorious."

# THE MUSIAD:

## A MINOR EPIC POEM.

*In the manner of Homer. A Fragment.*

IN ancient times, ere traps were fram'd,
　　Or cats in Britain's Ifle were known ;
A moufe, for pow'r and valour fam'd,
　　Poffefs'd in peace the regal throne.

A far-

A farmer's houfe he nightly ftorm'd,
   (In vain were bolts, in vain were keys ;)
The milk's fair furface he deform'd,
   And digg'd entrenchments in the cheefe.

In vain the farmer watch'd by night,
   In vain he fpread the poifon'd bacon ;
The moufe was wife as well as wight,
   Nor could by force or fraud be taken.

His fubjects follow'd where he led,
   And dealt deftruction all around;
His people, fhepherd-like, he fed ;
   Such mice are rarely to be found !

But evil fortune had decreed,
   (The foe of mice as well as men,)
The royal moufe at laft fhould bleed,
   Should fall---ne'er to arife again.

Upon

Upon a night, as authors fay,

   A lucklefs fcent our hero drew,

Upon forbidden ground to ftray,

   And pafs a narrow cranny through.|


That night a feaft the farmer made,

   And joy unbounded fill'd the houfe;

The fragments in the pantry fpread

   Afforded bus'nefs to the moufe.


He eat his fill, and back again

   Return'd; but accefs was deny'd.

He fcarch'd each corner, but in vain ;

   He found it clofe on every fide.


Let none our hero's fears deride ;

   He roar'd (ten mice of modern days,

As mice are dwindl'd and decay'd,

   So great a voice could fcarcely raife.)

                          Rouz'd

Rous'd at the voice, the farmer ran,
 And feiz'd upon his haplefs prey.
With entreaties the moufe began,
 And pray'rs, his anger to allay.


" O fpare my life," he trembling cries;
 " My fubjects will a ranfom give,
" Large as thy wifhes can devife,
 " Soon as it fhall be heard I live."


" No, wretch!" the farmer fays in wrath,
 " Thou dy'ft ; no ranfom I'll receive."
" My fubjects will revenge my death,"
 He faid; " this dying charge I leave."


The farmer lifts his armed hand,
 And on the moufe inflicts an wound.
What moufe could fuch a blow withftand?
 He fell, and dying bit the ground.

Thus

Thus LAMBR's fell, who flourish'd long,

    (I half forgot to tell his name ;)

But his renown lives in the song,

    And future times shall speak his fame.


A mouse, who walk'd about at large

    In safety, heard his mournful cries;

He heard him give his dying charge,

    And to the rest he frantic flies.


Thrice he essay'd to speak, and thrice

    Tears, such as mice may shed, fell down.

"Revenge your monarch's death," he cries,

    His voice half-stifl'd with a groan.


But having reassum'd his senses,

    And reason, such as mice may have,

He told out all the circumstances

    With many a strain and broken heave.

Chill'd

Chill'd with fad grief, th' affembly heard ;
   Each dropp'd a tear, and bow'd the head :
But fymptoms foon of rage appear'd,
   And vengeance for the royal dead.

Long fat they mute : at laft up rofe
   The great HYPENOR, blamelefs fage !
A hero born to many woes ;
   His head was filver'd o'er with age.

His bulk fo large, his joints fo ftrong,
   Though worn with grief, and paft his prime,
Few rats could equal him, 'tis fung,
   As rats are in thefe dregs of time.

Two fons, in battle brave, he had,
   Sprung from fair LALAGE's embrace ;
Short time they grac'd his nuptial bed,
   By dogs deftroy'd in cruel chafe.

                       Their

Their timelefs fate the mother wail'd,
 And pin'd with heart-corroding grief:
O'er every comfort it prevail'd,
 Till death advancing brought relief.

Now he's the laft of all his race,
 A prey to wo: He inly pin'd;
Grief pictur'd fat upon his face;
 Upon his breaft his head reclin'd.

And, " O my fellow-mice !" he faid,
 " Thefe eyes ne'er faw a day fo dire,
" Save when my gallant children bled.
 " O wretched fons! O wretched fire !

" But now a gen'ral caufe demands
 " Our grief, and claims our tears alone;
" Our monarch, flain by wicked hands,
 " No iffue left to fill the throne.

         " Yet

" Yet, tho' by hoftile man much wrong'd,

" My counfel is, from arms forbear,

" That fo your days may be prolong'd ;

" For man is Heav'n's peculiar care."

## L O C H L E V E N : A P O E M.

HAIL, native land ! where on the flow'ry banks
    Of LEVEN, Beauty ever-blooming dwells ;
A wreath of rofes, dropping with the dews
Of Morning, circles her ambrofial locks
Loofe-waving o'er her fhoulders ; where fhe treads,
Attendant on her fteps, the blufhing Spring
And Summer wait, to raife the various flow'rs
Beneath her footfteps ; while the cheerful birds
Carol their joy, and hail her as fhe comes,
Infpiring vernal love and vernal joy.

ATTEND, AGRICOLA ! who to the noife
Of public life preferr'ft the calmer fcenes
Of folitude, and fweet domeftic blifs,
Joys all thine own ! attend thy poet's ftrain,
Who triumphs in thy friendfhip, while he paints
The paft'ral mountains, the poetic ftreams,
Where raptur'd Contemplation leads thy walk,
While filent Evening on the plain defcends.


BETWEEN two mountains, whofe o'erwhelming

tops,

In their fwift courfe, arreft the bellying clouds,
A pleafant valley lies.   Upon the fouth,
A narrow op'ning parts the craggy hills ;
Thro' which the lake, that beautifies the vale,
Pours out its ample waters.   Spreading on,
And wid'ning by degrees, it ftretches north

To

To the high OCHEL, from whofe fnowy top

The ftreams that feed the lake flow thund'ring down.


THE twilight trembles o'er the mifty hills,

Trinkling with dews; and whilft the bird of day

Tunes his etherial note, and wakes the wood,

Bright from the crimfon curtains of the morn,

The fun appearing in his glory, throws

New robes of beauty over heav'n and earth.


O now, while nature fmiles in all her works,

Oft let me trace thy cowflip-cover'd banks,

O LEVEN! and the landfcape meafure round.

From gay KINROSS, whofe ftately tufted groves

Nod o'er the lake, tranfported let mine eye

Wander o'er all the various checquer'd fcene,

Of wilds, and fertile fields, and glitt'ring ftreams,

To ruin'd ARNOT; or afcend the height

OF

Of rocky LOMOND, where a riv'let pure

Burfts from the ground, and through the crumbled

 crags

Tinkles amufive. From the mountain's top,

Arouud me fpread, I fee the goodly fcene !

Inclofures green, that promife to the fwain

The future harveft ; many-colour'd meads ;

Irriguous vales, where cattle low, and fheep

That whiten half the hills ; fweet rural farms

Oft interfpers'd, the feats of paft'ral love

And innocence ; with many a fpiry dome

Sacred to heav'n, around whofe hallow'd walls

Our fathers flumber in the narrow houfe.

Gay, beauteous villas, bofom'd in the woods,

Like conftellations in the ftarry fky,

Complete the fcene. The vales, the vocal hills,

The woods, the waters, and the heart of man,

Send out a gen'ral fong ; 'tis beauty all

         To

To poet's eye, and mufic to his ear.


Nor is the fhepherd filent on his hill,

His flocks around ; nor fchool-boys, as they creep,

Slow pac'd, tow'rds fchool ; intent, with oaten pipe

They wake by turns wild mufic on the way.


Behold the man of forrows hail the light !

New rifen from the bed of pain, where late,

Tofs'd to and fro upon a couch of thorns,

He wak'd the long dark night, and wifh'd for morn.

Soon as he feels the quick'ning beam of heav'n,

And balmy breath of May, among the fields

And flow'rs he takes his morning walk : his heart

Beats with new life ; his eye is bright and blithe ;

Health ftrews her rofes o'er his cheek ; renew'd

In youth and beauty, his unbidden tongue

Pours native harmony, and fings to Heav'n.

Is

In ancient times, as ancient Bards have fung,
This was a foreft.  Here the mountain-oak
Hung o'er the craggy cliff, while from its top
The eagle mark'd his prey ; the ftately afh
Rear'd high his nervous ftature, while below
The twining alders darken'd all the fcene.
Safe in the fhade, the tenants of the wood
Affembled, bird and beaft.  The turtle-dove
Coo'd, amorous, all the livelong fummer's day.
Lover of men, the piteous redbreaft plain'd,
Sole-fitting on the bough.  Blithe on the bufh,
The blackbird, fweeteft of the woodland choir,
Warbled his liquid lay ;  to fhepherd-fwain
Mellifluous mufic, as his mafter's flock,
With his fair miftrefs and his faithful dog,
He tended in the vale :  while leverets round,
In fportive races, through the foreft flew
With feet of wind ; and, vent'ring from the rock,

The

The fnow-white coney fought his ev'ning meal.

Here, too, the poet, as infpir'd at eve

He roam'd the dufky wood, or fabled brook

That piece-meal printed ruins in the rock,

Beheld the blue-eyed Sifters of the ftream,

And heard the wild note of the fairy throng

That charm'd the Queen of heav'n, as round the tree

Time-hallow'd, hand in hand they led the dance,

With fky-blue mantles glitt'ring in her beam.

Low by the lake, as yet without a name,

Fair bofom'd in the bottom of the vale,

Arofe a cottage, green with ancient turf,

Half hid in hoary trees, and from the north

Fenc'd by a wood, but open to the Sun.

Here dwelt a peafant, rev'rend with the locks

Of age, yet youth was ruddy on his cheek;

His farm his only care; his fole delight

To

'To tend his daughter, beautiful and young,

To watch her paths, to fill her lap with flow'rs,

'To fee her fpread into the bloom of years,

The perfect picture of her mother's youth.

His age's hope, the apple of his eye,

Belov'd of Heav'n, his fair LEVINA grew

In youth and grace, the NAIAD of the vale.

Frefh as the flow'r amid the funny fhow'rs

Of May, and blither than the bird of dawn,

Both rofes' bloom gave beauty to her cheek,

Soft-temper'd with a fmile. The light of heav'n,

And innocence, illum'd her virgin-eye,

Lucid and lovely as the morning ftar.

Her breaft was fairer than the vernal bloom

·Of valley-lily, op'ning in a fhow'r ;

Fair as the morn, and beautiful as May,

The glory of the year, when firft fhe comes

Array'd, all-beauteous, with the robes of heav'n,

And

And breathing fummer breezes ; from her locks

Shakes genial dews, and from her lap the flow'rs.

Thus beautiful fhe look'd ; yet fomething more,

And better far than beauty, in her looks

Appear'd : the maiden blufh of modefty ;

The fmile of cheerfulnefs, and fweet content ;

Health's frefheft rofe, the fun-fhine of the foul ;

Each height'ning each, effus'd o'er all her form

A namelefs grace, the Beauty of the Mind.

Thus finifh'd fair above her peers, fhe drew

The eyes of all the village, and inflam'd

The rival fhepherds of the neighb'ring dale,

Who laid the fpoils of Summer at her feet,

And made the woods enamour'd of her name.

But pure as buds before they blow, and ftill

A virgin in her heart, fhe knew not love ;

But all alone, amid her garden fair,

L

From

From morn to noon, from noon to dewy eve,

She ſpent her days ; her pleaſing taſk to tend

The flow'rs ; to lave them from the water-ſpring ;

To ope the buds with her enamour'd breath,

Rank the gay tribes, and rear them in the ſun.

In youth the index of maturer years,

Left by her ſchool-companions at their play,

She'd often wander in the wood, or roam

The wildernefs, in queſt of curious flow'r,

Or neſt of bird unknown, till eve approach'd,

And hem'd her in the ſhade.   To obvious ſwain,

Or woodman chanting in the greenwood glin,

She'd bring the beauteous ſpoils, and aſk their names.

Thus ply'd aſſiduous her delightful taſk,

Day after day, till ev'ry herb ſhe nam'd

That paints the robe of Spring, and knew the voice

Of every. warbler in the vernal wood.

HER

HER garden ftretch'd along the river-fide,

High up a funny bank : on either fide,

A hedge forbade the vagrant foot ; above,

An ancient foreft fcreen'd the green recefs.

Tranfplanted here by her creative hand,

Each herb of Nature, full of fragrant fweets,

That fcents the breath of fummer ; every flow'r,

Pride of the plain, that blooms on feftal days

In fhepherd's garland, and adorns the year,

In beauteous clufters flourifh'd ; Nature's work,

And order, finifh'd by the hand of Art.

Here gowans, natives of the village green,

To daifies grew.  The lilies of the field

Put on the robe they neither fow'd nor fpun.

Sweet-fmelling fhrubs and cheerful fpreading trees,

Unfrequent fcatter'd, as by Nature's hand,

Shaded the flower's, and to her EDEN drew

The earlieft concerts of the fpring, and all

The various mufic of the vocal year :

Retreat romantic ! Thus from early youth

Her life fhe led ; one fummer's day, ferene

And fair, without a cloud : like poet's dream

Of vernal landfcapes, of ELYSIAN vales,

And iflands of the bleft ; where, hand in hand,

Eternal Spring and Autumn rule the year,

And Love and Joy lead on immortal youth.


'Twas on a fummer's day, when early fhow'rs

Had wak'd the various vegetable race

To life and beauty, fair LEVINA ftray'd.

Far in the blooming wildernefs fhe ftray'd

To gather herbs, and the fair race of flow'rs,

That Nature's hand creative pours at will,

Beauty unbounded ! over Earth's green lap,

Gay without number, in the day of rain.

O'er valleys gay, o'er hilloc's green fhe walk'd,

Sweet as the feafon, and at times awak'd
The echoes of the vale, with native notes
Of heart-felt joy, in numbers heav'nly fweet ;
Sweet as th' hofannahs of a Form of light,
A fweet-tongu'd Seraph in the bow'rs of blifs.

HER, as fhe halted on a green hill-top,
A quiver'd hunter fpied.   Her flowing locks,
In golden ringlets glitt'ring to the fun,
Upon her bofom play'd : her mantle green,
Like thine, O Nature ! to her rofy cheek
Lent beauty new ; as from the verdant leaf
The rofe-bud blufhes with a deeper bloom,
Amid the walks of May.   The ftranger's eye
Was caught as with etherial prefence.   Oft
He look'd to heav'n, and oft he met her eye
In all the filent eloquence of love ;
Then, wak'd from wonder, with a fmile began :

" Fair

" Fair wanderer of the wood! What heav'nly Pow'r,

Or Providence, conducts thy wand'ring fteps

To this wild foreft, from thy native feat

And parents, happy in a child fo fair ?

A fhepherdefs, or virgin of the vale,

Thy drefs befpeaks; but thy majeftic mien,

And eye, bright as the morning-ftar, confefs

Superior birth and beauty, born to rule :

As from the ftormy cloud of night, that veils

Her virgin-orb, appears the Queen of heav'n,

And with full beauty gilds the face of night.

Whom fhall I call the faireft of her fex,

And charmer of my foul ? In yonder vale,

Come, let us crop the rofes of the brook,

And wildings of the wood : Soft under fhade,

Let us recline by moffy fountain-fide,

While the wood fuffers in the beam of ncon.

I'll bring my love the choice of all the fhades;

Firſt fruits; the apple ruddy from the rock ;

And cluſt'ring nuts, that burniſh in the beam.

O wilt thou blefs my dwelling, and become

The owner of thefe fields ?   I'll give thee all

That I poffefs, and all thou feeſt is mine."


Thus fpoke the youth, with rapture in his eye,

And thus the maiden, with a bluſh began :

" Beyond the ſhadow of thefe mountains green,

Deep-bofom'd in the vale, a cottage ſtands,

The dwelling of my ſire, a peaceful fwain ;

Yet at his frugal board Health ſits a gueſt,

And fair Contentment crowns his hoary hairs,

The patriarch of the plains : 'ne'er by his door

The needy pafs'd, or the way-faring man.

His only daughter, and his only joy,

I feed my father's flock ; and, while they reſt,

At times retiring, lofe me in the wood,

Skill'd

Skill'd in the virtues of each fecret herb

That opes its virgin bofom to the Moon.

No flow'r amid the garden fairer grows

Than the fweet lily of the lowly vale,

The Queen of flowers —But fooner might the weed

That blooms and dies, the being of a day,

Prefume to match with yonder mountain oak,

That ftands the tempeft and the bolt of heav'n,

From age to age the monarch of the wood——

O ! had you been a fhepherd of the dale,

To feed your flock befide me, and to reft

With me at noon in thefe delightful fhades,

I might have lift'ned to the voice of love,

Nothing reluctant ; might with you have walk'd

Whole fummer-funs away.   At even-tide,

When heav'n and earth in all their glory fhine

With the laft fmiles of the departing fun ;

When the fweet breath of Summer feafts the fenfe,

And

And fecret pleafure thrills the heart of man ;
We might have walk'd alone, in conve.fe fweet,
Along the quiet vale, and woo'd the Moon
To hear the mufic of true lovers vows.

But fate forbids, and fortune's potent frown,
And honour, inmate of the noble breaft.
Ne'er can this hand in wedlock join with thine.
Ceafe, beauteous ftranger! ceafe, beloved youth!
To vex a heart that never can be yours."

Thus fpoke the maid, deceitful : but her eyes,
Beyond the partial purpofe of her tongue,
Perfuafion gain'd.   The deep-enamour'd youth
Stood gazing on her charms, and all his foul  ·
Was loft in love.   He grafp'd her trembling hand,
And breath'd the fofteft, the fincereft vows
Of love :   " O virgin! faireft of the fair !
My one beloved! Were the Scottifh throne

To me tranſmitted thro' a ſcepter'd line
Of anceſtors, thou, thou ſhould'ſt be my queen,
And CALEDONIA's diadems adorn
A fairer head than ever wore a crown."

SHE redden'd like the morning, under veil
Of her own golden hair.  The woods among,
They wander'd up and down with fond delay,
Nor mark'd the fall of ev'ning ; parted then,
The happieſt pair on whom the ſun declin'd.

NEXT day he found her on a flow'ry bank,
Half under ſhade of willows, by a ſpring,
The mirrour of the ſwains, that o'er the meads,
Slow-winding, ſcatter'd flow'rets in its way.
Thro' many a winding walk and alley green,
She led him to her garden.  Wonder-ſtruck,
He gaz'd, all eye, o'er th' enchanting ſcene :

And

And much he prais'd the walks, the groves, the
    flow'rs,
Her beautiful creation; much he prais'd
The beautiful creatrefs; and awak'd
The echo in her praife. Like the firft pair,
ADAM and EVE, in EDEN's blifsful bow'rs,
When newly come from their Creator's hand,
Our lovers liv'd in joy. Here, day by day,
In fond endearments, in embraces fweet,
That lovers only know, they liv'd, they lov'd,
And found the paradife that ADAM loft.
Nor did the virgin, with falfe modeft pride,
Retard the nuptial morn: fhe fix'd the day
That blefs'd the youth, and open'd to his eyes
An age of gold, the heav'n of happinefs
That lovers in their lucid moments dream.

AND

AND now the morning, like a rosy bride
Adorned on her day, put on her robes,
Her beauteous robes of light: the Naiad streams,
Sweet as the cadence of a poet's song,
Flow'd down the dale: the voices of the grove,
And ev'ry winged warbler of the air,
Sung over head, and there was joy in heav'n.
Ris'n with the dawn, the bride and bridal-maids
Stray'd thro' the woods, and o'er the vales, in quest
Of flow'rs, and garlands, and sweet-smelling herbs,
To strew the bridegroom's way, and deck his bed.

FAIR in the bosom of the level lake
Rose a green island, cover'd with a spring
Of flow'rs perpetual, goodly to the eye,
And blooming from afar. High in the midst,
Between two fountains, an enchanted tree
Grew ever green, and every month renew'd

Its

Its blooms and apples of Hesperian gold,

Here ev'ry bride (as ancient poets sing)

Two golden apples gather'd from the bough,

To give the bridegroom in the bed of love,

The pledge of nuptial concord and delight

For many a coming year.  LEVINA now

Had reach'd the isle, with an attendant maid,

And pull'd the mystic apples, pull'd the fruit ;

But wish'd and long'd for the enchanted tree.

Not fonder sought the first created fair

The fruit forbidden of the mortal tree,

The source of human wo.  Two plants arose

Fair by the mother's side, with fruits and flow'rs

In miniature.  One, with audacious hand,

In evil hour she rooted from the ground.

At once the island shook, and shrieks of wo

At times were heard, amid the troubled air.

Her whole frame shook, the blood forsook her face,

Her

Her knees knock'd, and her heart within her dy'd.

Trembling, and pale, and boding woes to come,

They feiz'd the boat, and hurried from the ifle.


And now they gain'd the middle of the lake,

And faw th' approaching land: now, wild with joy,

They row'd, they flew. When lo! at once effus'd,

Sent by the angry demon of the ifle,

A whirlwind rofe: it lafh'd the furious lake

To tempeft, overturn'd the boat, and funk

The fair LEVINA to a wat'ry tomb.

Her fad companions, bending from a rock,

Thrice faw her head, and fupplicating hands

Held up to heav'n, and heard the fhriek of death:

Then over-head the parting billow clos'd,

And op'd no more. Her fate in mournful lays,

The Mufe relates; and fure each tender maid

For her fhall heave the fympathetic figh,

And

And happ'ly my EUMELIA, (for her foul

Is pity's felf,) as, void of houfchold cares,

Her ev'ning walk fhe bends befide the lake, !

Which yet retains her name, fhall fadly drop

A tear, in mem'ry of the haplefs maid,

And mourn with me the forrows of the youth,

Whom from his miftrefs death did not divide.

Robb'd of the calm poffeffion of his mind,

All night he wander'd by the founding fhore,

Long looking o'er the lake, and faw at times

The dear, the dreary ghoft of her he lov'd;

Till love and grief fubdu'd his manly prime,

And brought his youth with forrow to the grave.


I KNEW an aged fwain, whofe hoary head

Was bent with years, the village-chronicle,

Who much had feen, and from the former times

Much had receiv'd. He, hanging o'er the hearth

In

In winter ev'nings, to the gaping swains,

And children circling round the fire, would tell

Stories of old, and tales of other times.

Of LOMOND and LEVINA he would talk;

And how of old, in BRITAIN's evil days,

When brothers against brothers drew the sword

Of civil rage, the hostile hand of war

Ravag'd the land, gave cities to the sword,

And all the country to devouring fire.

Then these fair forests and ELYSIAN scenes,

In one great conflagration, flam'd to heav'n.

Barren and black, by swift degrees arose

A muirish fen; and hence the lab'ring hind,

Digging for fuel, meets the mould'ring trunks

Of oaks, and branchy antlers of the deer.


Now sober Industry, illustrious Power!

Hath rais'd the peaceful cottage, calm abode

Of Innocence and Joy: now, sweating, guides

The shining ploughshare ; tames the stubborn soil ;

Leads the long drain along th' unfertile marsh ;

Bids the bleak hill with vernal verdure bloom,

The haunt of flock's : and clothes the barren heath

With waving harvests, and the golden grain.

Fair from his hand, behold the village rise,

In rural pride, 'mong intermingled trees !

Above whose aged tops, the joyful swains

At even-tide, descending from the hill,

With eye enamour'd, mark the many wreaths

Of pillar'd smoke, high-curling to the clouds.

The street resounds with Labour's various voice,

Who whistles at his work.  Gay on the green,

Young blooming boys, and girls with golden hair,

Trip nimble-footed, wanton in their play,

The village hope.  All in a rev'rend row,

Their gray-hair'd grandsires, sitting in the sun,

N                                      Before

Before the gate, and leaning on the ftaff,
The well-remember'd ftories of their youth
Recount, and fhake their aged locks with joy.

How fair a profpect rifes to the eye,
Where beauty vies in all her vernal forms,
For ever pleafant, and for ever new !
Swells th' exulting thought, expands the foul,
Drowning each ruder care : a blooming train
Of bright ideas rufhes on the mind.
Imagination roufes at the fcene,
And backward, thro' the gloom of ages paft,
Beholds ARCADIA, like a rural Queen,
Encircled with her fwains and rofy nymphs,
The mazy dance conducting on the green.
Nor yield to old ARCADIA's blifsful vales
Thine, gentle LEVEN ! green on either hand
Thy meadows fpread, unbroken of the plough,

With

With beauty all their own. Thy fields rejoice

With all the riches of the golden year.

Fat on the plain and mountain's funny fide,

Large droves of oxen, and the fleecy flocks

Feed undifturb'd, and fill the echoing air

With mufic, grateful to the mafter's ear.

The trav'ller ftops, and gazes round and round

O'er all the fcenes, that animate his heart

With mirth and mufic. Even the mendicant,

Bowbent with age, that on the old grey ftone,

Sole fitting, funs him in the public way,

Feels his heart leap, and to himfelf he fings.


How beautiful around the lake outfpreads

Its wealth of waters, the furrounding vales

Renews, and holds a mirrour to the fky,

Perpetual fed by many fifter-ftreams,

Haunts of the angler ! Firft, the gulfy Po,

N 2          That

That thro' the quaking marfh and waving reeds
Creeps flow and filent on. The rapid QUEECH,
Whofe foaming torrents o'er the broken fteep
Burft down impetuous, with the placid wave
Of flow'ry LEVEN, for the canine pike
And filver eel renown'd. But chief thy ftream,
O GAIRNY ! fweetly winding, claims the fong.
Firft on thy banks the DORIC reed I tun'd,
Stretch'd on the verdant grafs ; while twilight meek,
Enrob'd in mift, flow-failing thro' the air,
Silent and ftill, on ev'ry clofed flow'r
Shed drops nectareous ; and around the fields
No noife was heard, fave where the whifp'ring reeds
Wav'd to the breeze, or in the dufky air
The flow-wing'd crane mov'd heav'ly o'er the lee,
And fhrilly clamour'd as he fought his neft.
There would I fit, and tune fome youthful lay,
Or watch the motion of the living fires,

That

That day and night their never-ceafing courfe

Wheel round th' eternal poles, and bend the knee

To him the Maker of yon ftarry fky,

Omnipotent ! who, thron'd above all heav'ns,

Yet ever prefent through the peopl'd fpace

Of vaft Creation's infinite extent,

Pours life, and blifs, and beauty, pours himfelf,

His own effential goodnefs, o'er the minds

Of happy beings, thro' ten thoufand worlds.


Nor fhall the Mufe forget thy friendly heart,

O Lelius ! partner of my youthful hours ;

How often, rifing from the bed of peace,

We would walk forth to meet the fummer morn,

Inhaling health and harmony of mind ;

Philofophers and friends ; while fcience beam'd,

With ray divine as lovely on our minds

As yonder orient fun, whofe welcome light

Reveal'd

Reveal'd the vernal landscape to the view.

Yet oft, unbending from more serious thought,

Much of the loofer follies of mankind,

Hum'rous and gay, we'd talk, and much would laugh ;

While, ever and anon, their foibles vain

Imagination offer'd to our view.

FRONTING where GAIRNY pours his silent urn

Into the lake, an island lifts its head,

Grassy and wild, with ancient ruin heap'd

Of cells ; where from the noisy world retir'd

Of old, as fame reports, Religion dwelt

Safe from the insults of the dark'ned crowd

That bow'd the knee to ODIN ; and in times

Of ignorance, when CALEDONIA's sons

(Before the triple-crowned giant fell)

Exchang'd their simple faith for ROME's deceits.

Here

Here Superstition for her cloister'd sons
A dwelling rear'd, with many an arched vault;
Where her pale vot'ries at the midnight-hour,
In many a mournful strain of melancholy,
Chanted their orisons to the cold moon.
It now resounds with the wild-shrieking gull,
The crested lapwing, and the clamorous mew,
The patient heron, and the bittern dull,
Deep-founding in the base, with all the tribe
That by the water seek th' appointed meal.

From hence the shepherd in the fenced fold,
'Tis said, has heard strange sounds, and music wild;
Such as in SELMA, by the burning oak
Of hero fallen, or of battle lost,
Warn'd FINGAL's mighty son, from trembling chords
Of untouch'd harp, self-founding in the night.
Perhaps th' afflicted Genius of the lake,

That

That leaves the wat'ry grot, each night to mourn

The wafte of time, his defolated ifles

And temples in the duft : his plaintive voice

Is heard refounding thro' the dreary courts

Of high LOCHLEVEN caftle, famous once,

Th' abode of heroes of the BRUCE's line ;

Gothic the pile, and high the folid walls,

With warlike ramparts, and the ftrong defence

Of jutting battlements, an age's toil !

No more its arches echo to the noife

Of joy and feftive mirth.   No more the glance

Of blazing taper thro' its windows beams,

And quivers on the undulating wave :

But naked ftand the melancholy walls,

Lafh'd by the wintry tempefts, cold and bleak,

That whiftle mournful thro' the empty halls,

And piece-meal crumble down the tow'rs to duft.

Perhaps in fome lone, dreary, defert tower,

That

That time has fpar'd, forth from the window looks,

Half hid in grafs, the folitary fox ;

While from above the owl, mufician dire !

Screams hideous, harfh, and grating to the ear.

Equal in age, and fharers of its fate,

A row of mofs-grown trees around it ftand.

Scarce here and there, upon their blafted tops,

A fhrivell'd leaf diftinguifhes the year ;

Emblem of hoary age, the eve of life,

When man draws nigh his everlafting home,

Within a ftep of the devouring grave ;

When all his views and tow'ring hopes are gone,

And ev'ry appetite before him dead.

Bright fhines the morn, while in the ruddy caft

The fun hangs hov'ring o'er th' Atlantic wave.

Apart on yonder green hill's funny fide,

Seren'd with all the mufic of the morn,

O                    Attentive

Attentive let me fit ; while from the rock,

The fwains, laborious, roll the limeftone huge,

Bounding elaftic from th' indented grafs,

At every fall it fprings, and thund'ring fhoots,

O'er rocks and precipices, to the plain.

And let the fhepherd careful tend his flock

Far from the dang'rous fteep; nor, O ye fwains!

Stray heedlefs of its rage.   Behold the tears

Yon wretched widow o'er the mangled corpfe

Of her dead hufband pours, who, haplefs man!

Cheerful and ftrong went forth at rifing morn

To ufual toil ; but, ere the evening hour,

His fad companions bare him lifelefs home.

Urg'd from the hill's high top, with progrefs fwift,

A weighty ftone, refiftlefs, rapid came,

Seen by the fated wretch, who ftood unmov'd,

Nor turn'd to fly, till flight had been in vain ;

When now arriv'd the inftrument of death,

-And

And fell'd him to the ground.  The thirfty land

Drank up his blood : fuch was the will of Heav'n.


How wide the landfcape opens to the view !

Still as I mount, the lefs'ning hills decline,

Till high above them northern GRAMPIUS lifts

His hoary head, bending beneath a load

Of everlafting fnow.   O'er fouthern fields

I fee the CHEVIOT hills, the ancient bounds

Of two contending kingdoms.   There in fight·

Brave PIERCY and the gallant DOUGLAS bled,

The houfe of heroes, and the death of hofts !

Wat'ring the fertile fields, majeftic FORTH,

Full, deep, and wide, rolls placid to the fea,

With many a veffel trim and oared bark

In rich profufion cover'd, wafting o'er

The wealth and product of far diftant lands.

O 2

But chief mine eye on the fubjected vale

Of Leven pleas'd looks down ; while o'er the trees,.

That fhield the hamlet with the fhade of years,

The tow'ring fmoke of early fire afcends,

And the fhrill cock proclaims th' advanced morn.


How blefl the man! who, in thefe peaceful plains,

Ploughs his paternal field ; far from the noife,

The care, and buftle of a bufy world.

All in the facred, fweet, fequefter'd vale

Of Solitude, the fecret primrofe-path

Of rural life, he dwells ; and with him dwells

Peace and Content, twins of the Sylvan fhade,

And all the Graces of the golden age.

Such is Agricola, the wife, the good,

By nature formed for the calm retreat,

The filent path of life. Learn'd, but not fraught

With

With felf-importance, as the ftarched fool ;

Who challenges refpect by folemn face,

By ftudied accent, and high-founding phrafe.

Enamour'd of the fhade, but not morofe.

Politenefs, rais'd in courts by frigid rules,

With him fpontaneous grows.   Not books alone,

But man his ftudy, and the better part ;

To tread the ways of virtue, and to act

The various fcenes of life with GOD's applaufe.

Deep in the bottom of the flow'ry vale,

With blooming fallows and the leafy twine

Of verdant alders fenc'd, his dwelling ftands

Complete in rural elegance.   The door,

By which the poor or pilgrim never pafs'd,

Still open, fpeaks the mafter's bounteous heart.

There, O how fweet ! amid the fragrant fhrubs

At ev'ning cool to fit ; while, on their boughs,

The nefted fongfters twitter o'er their young,

And

And the hoarfe low of folded cattle breaks

The filence, wafted o'er the fleeping lake,

Whofe waters glow beneath the purple tinge

Of weftern cloud ; while converfe fweet deceives

The ftealing foot of time. Or where the ground,

Mounded irregular, points out the graves

Of our forefathers, and the hallow'd fane,

Where fwains affembling worfhip, let us walk,

In foftiy-foothing melancholy thought,

As Night's feraphic bard, immortal YOUNG,

Or fweet-complaining GREY ; there fee the goal

Of human life, were drooping, faint, and tir'd,

Oft mifs'd the prize, the weary racer refts.


THUS fung the youth, amid unfertile wilds

And namelefs deferts, unpoetic ground !

Far from his friends he ftray'd, recording thus

The dear remembrance of his native fields,

To

To cheer the tedious night ; while flow difeafe

Prey'd on his pining vitals, and the blafts

Of dark DECEMBER fhook his humble cot.


## O D E :

### . T O   P A O L I.

WHAT man, what hero fhall the Mufes fing,

    On claffic lyre or CALEDONIA ftring,

      Whofe name fhall fill th' immortal page ;

Who, fir'd from heav'n with energy divine,

In fun-bright glory bids his actions fhine

      Firft in the annals of the age ?

    Ceas'd are the golden times of yore ;

    The age of heroes is no more ;

Rare, in thefe latter times, arife to fame

The poet's ftrain infpir'd, or hero's heav'nly flame.

                What

## II.

What ſtar ariſing in the ſouthern ſky,

New to the heav'ns, attracting EUROPE's eye,

 With beams unborrow'd ſhines afar ?

Who comes, with thouſands marching in his reai,

Shining in arms, ſhaking his bloody ſpear,

 Like the red comet, ſign of war ?

 PAOLI ! ſent of heav'n, to ſave

 A riſing nation of the brave ;

Whoſe firm right hand his angels arm, to bear

A ſhield before his hoſt, and dart the bolts of war.

## III.

He comes ! he comes ! the ſaviour of the land !

His drawn ſword flames in his uplifted hand,

 Enthuſiaſt in his country's cauſe ;

Whoſe firm reſolve obeys a nation's call,

To riſe deliverer, or a martyr fall

 To Liberty, to dying laws.

Ye fons of Freedom ! fing his praife ;

Ye poets ! bind his brows with bays ;

Ye fcepter'd fhadows ! caſt your honours down,

And bow before the head that never wore a crown.

## IV.

Who to the hero can the palm refufe ?

Great ALEXANDER ſtill the world fubdues,

 The heir of everlafting praife.

But when the hero's flame, the patriot's light ;

When virtues human and divine unite ;

 When olives twine among the bays,

 And, mutual, both MINERVA's ſhine ;

 A conſtellation fo divine,

A wond'ring world behold, admire, and love,

And his beſt image here, th' Almighty marks above.

## V.

As the lone fhepherd hides him in the rocks,

When high heav'n thunders ; as the tim'rous flocks

     P      From

From the defcending torrent flee :

So flies a world of flaves at War's alarms,

When Zeal on flame, and Liberty in arms,

 Leads on the fearlefs and the free,

 Refiftlefs ; as the torrent flood,

 Horn'd like the moon, uproots the wood,

Sweeps flocks, and herds, and harvefts from their bafe,

And moves th' eternal hills from their appointed place.

### VI.

Long haft thou labour'd in the glorious ftrife,

O land of Liberty ! profufe of life,

 And prodigal of pricelefs blood.

Where heroes bought with blood the martyr's crown,

A race arofe, heirs of their high renown,

 Who dar'd their fate thro' fire and flood:

 And GAFFORI the great arofe,

 Whofe words of pow'r, difarm'd his foes ;

And where the filial image fmil'd afar,

The fire turn'd not afide the thunders of the war.

## VII.

O Liberty! to man a guardian giv'n,
Thou beſt and brighteſt attribute of heav'n!

 From whom deſcending, thee we ſing.

By nature wild, or by the arts refin'd,
We feel thy pow'r eſſential to our mind;

 Each ſon of Freedom is a king.

Thy praiſe the happy world proclaim,

 And BRITAIN worſhips at thy name,

Thou guardian angel of BRITANNIA's iſle!
And GOD and man rejoice in thy immortal ſmile.

## VIII.

Iſland of beauty! lift thy head on high;
Sing a new ſong of triumph to the ſky!

 The day of thy deliv'rance ſprings!

The day of vengeance to thy ancient foe.
Thy ſons ſhall lay the proud oppreſſor low,

 And break the head of tyrant kings.

P 2

PAOLI!

PAOLI! mighty man of war!

All bright in arms, thy conqu'ring car

Afcend; thy people from the foe redeem,

Thou delegate of Heav'n, and fon of the Supreme!

### IX.

Rul'd by th' eternal laws, fupreme o'er all,

Kingdoms, like kings, fucceffive rife and fall.

When CÆSAR conquer'd half the earth,

And fpread his eagles in Britannia's fun,

Did CÆSAR dream the favage huts he won

Should give a far-fam'd kingdom birth?

That here fhould ROMAN Freedom 'light;

The weftern Mufes wing their flight;

The Arts, the Graces find their fav'rite home;

Our armies awe the globe, and BRITAIN rival ROME?

### X.

Thus, if th' Almighty fay, " Let Freedom be,"

Thou, CORSICA! thy golden age fhalt fee.

Rejoice

Rejoice with fongs, rejoice with fmiles;

Worlds yet unfound, and ages yet unborn,

Shall hail a new BRITANNIA in her morn,

The Queen of arts, the Queen of ifles:

The Arts, the beauteous train of Peace,

Shall rife and rival ROME and GREECE;

A NEWTON Nature's book unfold fublime;

A MILTON fing to heav'n, and charm the ear of Time.

# O D E:

## TO THE CUCKOW.

### I.

HAIL, beauteous Stranger of the wood,

Attendant on the fpring!

Now heav'n repairs thy rural feat,

And woods thy welcome fing.

## II.

Soon as the daisie decks the green,
    Thy certain voice we hear:
Haft thou a ftar to guide thy path,
    Or mark the rolling year?

## III.

Delightful Vifitant! with thee
    I hail the time of flow'rs,
When heav'n is fill'd with mufic fweet
    Of birds among the bow'rs.

## IV.

The fchoolboy, wand'ring in the wood
    To pull the flow'rs fo gay,
Starts, thy curious voice to hear,
    And imitates thy lay.

## V.

Soon as the pea puts on the bloom,
  Thou fly'ft thy vocal vale,
An annual gueft, in other lands,
  Another fpring to hail.

## VI.

Sweet bird! thy bow'r is ever green,
  Thy fky is ever clear;
Thou haft no forrow in thy fong,
  No winter in thy year!

## VII.

O could I fly, I'd fly with thee:
  We'd make, with focial wing,
Our annual vifit o'er the globe,
  Companions of the fpring.

# ELEGY:

## TO SPRING.

### I.

'TIS paſt : the iron North has ſpent his rage ;

 Stern Winter now reſigns the length'ning day ;

The ſtormy howlings of the winds aſſwage,

 And warm o'er ether weſtern breezes play.

### II.

Of genial heat and cheerful light the ſource,

 From ſouthern climes, beneath another ſky,

The ſun, returning, wheels his golden courſe ;

 Before his beams all noxious vapours fly.

### III.

Far to the north grim Winter draws his train

 To his own clime, to ZEMBLA's frozen ſhore ;

Where, thrón'd on ice, he holds eternal reign ;

 Where whirlwinds madden, and where tempeſts roar.

Loos'd

### IV.

Loos'd from the bands of froft, the verdant ground
    Again puts on her robe of cheerful green,
Again puts forth her flow'rs ; and all around,
    Smiling, the cheerful face of Spring is feen.

### V.

Behold ! the trees new-deck their wither'd boughs ;
    Their ample leaves the hofpitable plane,
The taper elm, and lofty afh difclofe ;
    The blooming hawthorn variegates the fcene.

### VI.

The lily of the vale, of flow'rs the Queen,
    Puts on the robe fhe neither few'd nor fpun :
The birds on ground, or on the branches green,
    Hop to and fro, and glitter in the fun.

Q                        Soon

### VII.

Soon as o'er eaftern hills the morning peers,
   From her low neft the tufted lark upfprings ;
And, cheerful finging, up the air fhe fteers ;
   Still high fhe mounts, ftill loud and fweet fhe fings.

### VIII.

On the green furze, cloth'd o'er with golden blooms
   That fill the air with fragrance all around,
The linet fits, and tricks his gloffy plumes,
   While o'er the wild his broken notes refound.

### IX.

While the fun journeys down the weftern fky,
   Along the greenfward, mark'd with ROMAN mound,
Beneath the blithefome fhepherd's watchful eye,
   The cheerful lambkins dance and frifk around.

                         Now

### X.

Now is the time for thofe who wifdom love,
　　Who love to walk in Virtue's flow'ry road,
Along the lovely paths of Spring to rove,
　　And follow Nature up to Nature's God.

### XI.

Thus Zoroasters ftudied Nature's laws;
　　Thus Socrates, the wifeft of mankind;
Thus heav'n-taught Plato trac'd th' Almighty caufe,
　　And left the wond'ring multitude behind.

### XII.

Thus Ashley gather'd Academic bays;
　　Thus gentle Thomson, as the Seafons roll,
Taught them to fing the great Creator's praife,
　　And bear their poet's name from pole to pole.

Q 2　　　　　　　Thus

## XIII.

Thus have I walk'd along the dewy lawn ;

   My frequent foot the blooming wild hath worn ;

Before the lark I've fung the beauteous dawn,

   And gather'd health from all the gales of morn.

## XIV.

And, even when Winter chill'd the aged year,

   I wander'd lonely o'er the hoary plain ;

Tho' frofty Boreas warn'd me to forbear,

   Boreas, with all his tempefts, warn'd in vain.

## XV.

Then fleep my nights, and quiet blefs'd my days ;

   I fear'd no lofs, my MIND was all my ftore ;

No anxious wifhes e'er difturb'd my eafe ;

   Heav'n gave content and health—I afk'd no more.

Now

### XVI.

Now Spring returns : but not to me returns
    The vernal joy my better years have known ;
Dim in my breaſt life's dying taper burns,
    And all the joys of life with health are flown.

### XVII.

Starting and ſhiv'ring in th' inconſtant wind,
    Meagre and pale, the ghoſt of what I was,
Beneath ſome blaſted tree I lie reclin'd,
    And count the ſilent moments as they paſs :

### XVIII.

The winged moments, whoſe unſtaying ſpeed
    No art can ſtop, or in their courſe arreſt ;
Whoſe flight ſhall ſhortly count me with the dead,
    And lay me down in peace with them that reſt.

 Oft

### XIX.

Oft morning-dreams prefage approaching fate ;
   And morning-dreams, as poet's tell, are true.
Led by pale ghofts, I enter Death's dark gate,
   And bid the realms of light and life adieu.

### XX.

I hear the helplefs wail, the fhriek of wo ;
   I fee the muddy wave, the dreary fhore,
The fluggifh ftreams that flowly creep below,
   Which mortals vifit, and return no more.

### XXI.

Farewell, ye blooming fields ! ye cheerful plains !
   Enough for me the church-yard's lonely mound,
Where Melancholy with ftill Silence reigns,
   And the rank grafs waves o'er the cheerlefs ground.

There

### XXII.

There let me wander at the ſhut of eve,

    When ſleep ſits dewy on the labourer's eyes,

The world and all its buſy follies leave,

    And talk with Wiſdom where my DAPHNIS lies.

### XXIII.

There let me ſleep forgotten in the clay,

    When death ſhall ſhut theſe weary aching eyes,

Reſt in the hopes of an eternal day,

    Till the long night's gone, and the loſt morn ariſe.

### FINIS.